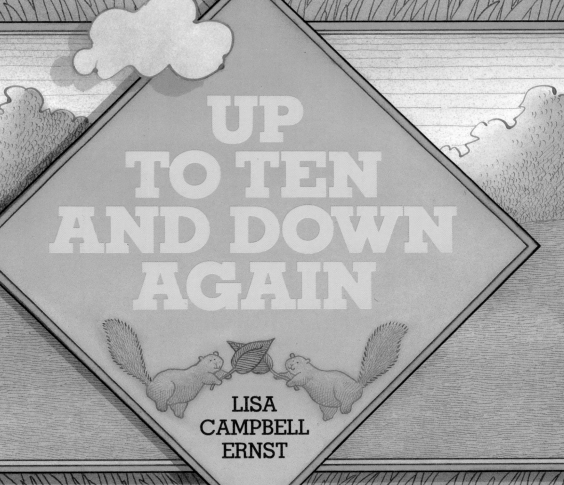

UP
TO TEN
AND DOWN
AGAIN

LISA
CAMPBELL
ERNST

A Mulberry
Paperback Book
· NEW YORK ·

For Kevin
and Marshall

The Library of Congress has cataloged the Lothrop, Lee & Shepard Books edition
of *Up to Ten and Down Again* as follows:
Ernst, Lisa Campbell.   Up to ten and down again.   ISBN 0-688-04541-3   ISBN 0-688-04542-1 (lib. bdg.)
1. Children's stories, American.   [1. Picnicking—Fiction. 2. Stories without words. 3. Counting.]
I. Title. PZ7.E7323Up   1986   [E]   84-21852   10 9 8 7 6 5 4 3 2 1
First Mulberry Edition, 1995   ISBN 0-688-14391-1

1

duck

2 cars

3
dogs

4
boys

5 girls

6
balls

7
boats

8
baskets

9
hats

10
clouds

10 clouds

9 hats

8 baskets

7

boats

6
balls

5
girls

4

boys

3 dogs

2 cars

1

duck